Little Mittens For The Little Darlings

Aunt Fanny

Copyright © 2023 Culturea Editions
Text and cover : © public domain
Edition : Culturea (Hérault, 34)
Contact : infos@culturea.fr
Print in Germany by Books on Demand
Design and layout : Derek Murphy
Layout : Reedsy (https://reedsy.com/)
ISBN : 9791041819706
Légal deposit : July 2023

Little Mittens For The Little Darlings
THE LITTLE KITTENS.

Only to think! A letter from Aunt Fanny to the little ones, which begins in this fanny way:

"YOU DARLING KITTENS—"

All the small children looked at Mary O'Reilly—who sat staring at the fire, with her whiskers sticking up in the air, and then felt their faces with their little fat hands. They did not find the least scrap of a whisker anywhere on their round cheeks; and Pet said—"But I a ittle girl; I not a kitty"—at which all the family laughed, and ran to kiss her—and she thought she had been very smart, I can tell you; and clapped her hands and said again—"No! I not a kitty!" and all the rest of the little ones said they were not kittens, and for two minutes there was such fun, everybody mewing like cats, and patting each other softly for play. The little mother said they must all have been to Catalonia; and that might be the reason why Aunt Fanny called them "kittens;" or perhaps it was because she loved them.

So she began again:

DARLING KITTENS—

You must have stories as well as the rest—of course you must. If I should forget to write some for such sweet little monkeys as you, that I know and love so dearly, and some other sweet little monkeys that I don't know, but love very much; why, Mr. Appleton, who has sweet little monkeys of his own, would say to me with a grave face—"Aunt Fanny! I'm surprised at you! What do you mean by such conduct? What has become of that big room in your heart, which you keep brimful of love for babies and little bits of children? Do you want them to sit humdrum on rainy days, when they are tired of playing with dolls, and tops, and kittens, and have no story book for their kind mammas to read to them? This will never do, Aunt Fanny. Please to begin right away!"

Oh! what a dreadful thing it would be, for any one to suppose that I did not love you any more. I could not bear it; so here I am beginning "right away," and the very first thing that comes into my mind is a story about kittens. What do you think of that! you lovely little red, white, and blue darlings! with your pretty red cheeks, pure white skins, and sweet blue eyes! The bright hazel, gray, and black eyes are like the stars; so no wonder we love the "star-spangled banner," when such precious little ones as you wear the very same colors as the dear old flag. Then —

"Hurrah for the children forever,And three cheers for the red, white, and blue."

And now for the kitten story.

One cold, bright day in the middle of last winter, a lady came to see me. She brought with her two little girls with the roundest and rosiest faces; even their dear little noses were red as roses for a minute or two, till they got warm, because Mr. Jack Frost had been pinching them all the way from their house to mine. But he couldn't get at their fingers, for they were covered with pretty white mittens, and they had on such warm coats and nice fur tippets, and so many cunning little flannel petticoats about a quarter of a yard long, that they looked as round as dumplings. Their fat legs were all packed up in woollen leggings; and they had little brown button-over boots — with, would you believe it? heels! Just to think of it! heels! and they didn't tumble down either. Well, I gave them — guess how many kisses, apiece? and then their mamma and I sat down to talk. It was very old kind of talk: all about "contrabands" (that's a very hard word, isn't it?) and about the best way to make noodle soup, and so on. The children did not care a fig about that kind of talk; so they walked off to a corner, and began to play with some funny things they found. One was an old man all made of black wadding, and another was a very fat old woman made of white wadding. The old woman hadn't the least speck of a foot to stand on; her body was just a great round roll of wadding, without legs; I never saw a real, live old woman without legs, did you? But this one must have come from no one knows where. You see, she and the black wadding man were left by Santa Claus one Christmas night, who drove off in his sleigh in such a hurry that he forgot even to leave a card with their names; and that's just the long and the short of it, or the black and the white of it.

Pretty soon Sarah, my daughter, came into the room. "Oh you dear, dear, little things!" she cried, "I am so glad to see you!"

"Then tell me a story," said Mary, the elder.

"Would you like to hear about the three little kittens that lost their mittens?"

"O yes, yes!" they both exclaimed.

Then Sarah took dear little Charlotte upon her lap, and Mary stood close to her knee, pressing lovingly against her; her large dark eyes were fastened on Sarah's face, for she did not mean to lose a single word of the delightful story; and Sarah began:

"Three little kittensLost their mittens;And they began to cry:'Oh mother dear,We very much fear,That we have lost our mittens.'"

"Oh, what bad kittens! I shame for them!" said Charlotte.

"Their mamma was 'shame' too," continued Sarah, "for she gave them a dab with her paw on their ears, and said in a severe voice:

"'Lost your mittens?Oh, you naughty kittens!Now you shan't have any pie!"

and then she gave them each such a good whipping that the tears ran down on the ground, and made it very damp.

"But the three little kittens,Found their mittens,And they began to cry,'Oh, mother dear,Only see here,See! just look! we have found our mittens.'"

"Oh! I so grad," said little Charlotte, and she clapped her hands; and then gazing at her own pretty white mittens, held them up, and cried: "Look! I've got mittens! look! look!"

"So you have," said Sarah, kissing her — "and they keep your hands nice and warm, don't they?"

"Did they keep the kittens' hands warm too?" asked little Mary.

"Yes, as warm as toast; and their mother was so glad they were found, that she hugged her three children to her breast, and cried:

"'Found your mittens?Oh, you dear, good little kittens!Now you shall have some pie.'

"Then she got a large apple pie out of the closet, and cut them a tremendous slice apiece; and the little kittens were so glad that they keptsaying, 'purr purr purr,' which meant, 'Thank you, ma'am! Oh, thank you, ma'am! Thank you very much.'

"But, dear me, what a pity! they forgot to take their mittens off; and such a sticky, lot, when they were done eating, you never saw! They were full of bits of apple, and sugar, and crumbs of buttery pie crust. The kittens stared with dismal faces at their mother, and it was plain to see that

"The three little kittensHad soiled their mittens;And they began to cry:'Oh, mother dear,We very much fear,That we have soiled our mittens.'

"This was really dreadful! The old cat started up, her whiskers curling with rage; she very nearly danced on her hind legs, she was so angry. It wasn't right to get into such a passion; but then you know she was only an old cat, and had not read that pretty verse which begins, 'Let dogs delight to bark and bite;' so she mewed, and snarled, and made her tail up into an arch, and said very crossly:

"'You've soiled your mittens?Oh! you naughty, bad kittens!'

And she whipped them so dreadfully this time, that they cried till the tears made a little puddle on the ground."

"Oh my!" said Charlotte, and her bright black eyes looked very sorry.

"Oh my!" said Mary, exactly like her little sister.

Sarah laughed a little bit, and said, "Oh my!" too. "Your dear mamma wouldn't do so, would she?" she asked.

"Oh no!" cried both the children; and then they had to get down, and run to kiss their mother; whose large dark eyes were full of love for her darlings.

"After the poor kittens had wiped their eyes, and blowed their noses, and sighed two or three times, one of them said to the others, "Don't cry any more. Let's get our little pails and fill them with water and borrow a piece of soap from the cook, and wash our mittens."

"'Oh yes! you darling sister, to think of such a nice plan!' cried the other two; and they rolled over on their backs, and flourished all their soft paws in the air together, they were so glad.

"So the three little kittensWashed their mittens,And hung them up to dry.

"Then they ran to their mother, who was fast asleep on the rug, with her tail curled round her; but they did not mind that—which I think was not quite polite—for when people and cats are taking a nap, everybody must keep very quiet, and not go near them or make a noise; but our friends, the kittens, did not think, you see: they just went pounce right on top of their mother, and sang out:

"'Oh, mother, dear,Only see here,See! open your eye, see! we have washed our mittens.'

"The old cat, for a wonder, did not get angry; instead of that, she smiled a sweet smile, rubbed her chin with her paw, and in a musical, mewing tone of delighted surprise, exclaimed:

"'Washed your mittens!Oh you little ducks of kittens!But s-hh! Listen! I think I hear a rat close by.'

"'Purr purr.'

"'Mew!' said one of the little kittens, who was afraid of the rat.

"'Hush up, you naughty little kitten! I hear a rat close by.'

"That's all."

"Oh!" cried Mary, "tell me about the rat, won't you?"

"Well, I believe the old cat ran like lightning after the rat, caught him, and gave her little kittens a paw apiece, and eat all the rest up herself."

"Every bit?" asked Charlotte.

"I don't think she left the least scrap," said Sarah.

"Tell another story," said Mary. "Ah, do!"

How we laughed—their mother and I—softly to ourselves, when Mary asked Sarah for more stories; Sarah laughed too, and was just going to begin another, when the mother said it was time to go. So I bid her good-by, and sent my kind regards to Mr. Ewer, the dear little childrens' father — who is a minister, and one of the best men in the whole world; because he is never tired of working for God. Great crowds of people go to hear him preach, and his constant prayer is: that he may bring them all, old and young, to the feet of the Blessed Jesus.

I was very sorry to have those sweet little pets go so soon, because I wanted to talk to them myself; but, of course, they must mind their mother; and I never tease any one to stay. It is not polite; so I kissed them heartily, and went with them to the front door.

The wind blew sharply in my face, and I said, "You dear little kits! I'm glad you are not made of sugar candy; you would snap all to pieces such a cold day! but here, what is this? where in the world is your mitten?"

There was the darling little Charlotte, standing in the cold, with only one white mitten on.

"Why dear me!" exclaimed her mother, "what have you done with it?"

Then the cunning precious pet laughed out merrily, and turning her sweet face up to us, with the funniest little twist of her eye, lisped out:

"I a ittie kitten,I loss my mitten."

We both burst out laughing—we could not help it; but her mother, smoothing the smiles almost away, made believe to be the kittens' mother, and cried out:

"Lost your mitten?Oh you naughty little kitten!Now you can't have any pie."

So back we all went to the parlor, both the children laughing, as if it was the funniest joke in the whole world; and we looked under the tables, and chairs, and sofas, and piano, and into all the corners. The little darlings, dancing up and down, and singing that they were little kittens, and had lost their mittens, and running all round the room in the greatest glee. But we could not find the mitten; and after we had stopped looking, and were feeling very sorry that Mr. Jack Frost would have such a fine chance pinching Charlotte's fingers, what do you think the queer little puss did? Why, she just crept behind the door, which was opened way back nearly to the wall, and in a minute, out she came again, with the lost mitten. The funny little thing had hidden it there on purpose, so as to be like the kittens in the story.

How we did laugh — for you know she was in play, and did not mean to do anything naughty. She skipped up to her mamma, and chirped out:

"See, mamma, dear!Only look here,I found my mitten! didn't I?"

And her mother just caught her up in her aims and kissed her, and said:

"Found your mitten?Oh, you good little kitten!Now you shall have some pie!"

And off they went, the children perfectly delighted with the comical play of the kittens. I dare say they hid their mittens again as soon as they got home. I know I should, if I had been a funny little girl; wouldn't you? But don't hide the soldiers' mittens — for all the world! They wouldn't like that at all, you know; and if any of them was as cross as the old cat, they might ask General McClellan to give them leave of absence, so that they could come and give you what Paddy gave the drum.

"What was that?"

"Rat-a-tat-tat!Rat-a-tat-tat!Rat-a-tat-tat-too!"

THE FOURTH COMMANDMENT.

One evening the little mother said: "Here is a sweet little story for the 'darling kittens'; but first Aunt Fanny requested me to ask Clara to repeat the fourth commandment to the little ones, slowly and distinctly."

"Yes, mamma," said Clara, "I will; I know it perfectly. Gentleman and ladies, come stand in a row before me."

So the little tots trotted and skipped up to their sister,—who was quite a great girl in their eyes—and after hopping up and down, first on one foot, then on the other, and puckering up their mouths like little bags, to keep all the laugh in tight, they stood almost still.

Then Clara all at once grew grave; for she was about to repeat something out of the Holy Bible, and although this was a great pleasure to her, she did not dream of even smiling.

She began thus, in a clear, distinct voice:

"Remember the Sabbath day, to keep it holy. Six days shalt thou labor and do all thy work; but the seventh day is the Sabbath of the Lord thy God: in it thou shalt not do any work, thou, nor thy son, nor thy daughter, thy man-servant, nor thy maid-servant, nor thy cattle, nor the stranger that is within thy gates. For in six days the Lord made heaven and earth, the sea, and all that in them is, and rested the seventh day: wherefore the Lord blessed the Sabbath day, and hallowed it."

The little ones had listened with great attention, and their mother now said:

"My darlings, you know it is wrong to work on Sunday. You see me put all my sewing out of the way on Saturday evenings, and on Sunday I go to church; and when I am home, I either read the Holy Bible or a good book, or talk to you. You are very little children, but if you saw any one sewing or working on Sunday, what would you say to them?"

"'Member the Sabbath day," chimed the little ones.

"That's right! and you too must never forget to 'keep it holy.' This little story is about keeping the fourth commandment; and now I will read it:

"Once upon a time, a pretty little girl was riding in a stage coach, along a country road, with her aunt. She had been making this aunt a visit, and was now coming home to her kind mother. It was a pretty long ride, over hill and dale; but Tillie, for that was the little girl's name, was delighted at first, and laughed every time the stones in the road made the stage give a jump, and a bump, and a rumble, and a tumble.

"But pretty soon she began to get tired, and wanted to jump and tumble herself. She could not run about in a stage coach — of course not — there was no room; and Tillie's little feet began to kick, because they could not get any play.

"At last her aunt said, 'Sit still, dear: look at the ducks, and pigs, and geese all along the road; and see those patient oxen in the field, how they turn one way when the farmer says "Gee," and the other when he says "Haw."'

"Tillie looked for a moment, and then said, 'Oh, I so tired.' Just then she spied a large black and white blanket shawl lying on her aunt's lap. She took it, and with great efforts managed to roll it up, and fasten the roll with two large pins she found in it, which had shiny black heads. Then she made believe that the shawl was a baby; and very soon every one in the stage was laughing at her funny talk.

"'Oh, my dear baby,' she said, 'I 'fraid the light hurts your little eyes; please, auntie, lend me your veil.'

"Her aunt smiled, and gave Tillie her brown barege veil; and the little girl spread it tenderly over the top of the shawl, saying, 'There, my baby, don't cry any more.'

"'Ai! ai! ai! a——i!' screamed the baby—that is, Tillie screamed, and pretended it was her—'ai! ai! a——i!'

"'What, darling, what is it?' said Tillie, 'do you want to look out of the window and see the pretty trees? So you shall, dearest. There, don't bump your little head!' And taking off the brown barege veil, she poked the top of the shawl out of the window; and it had a real nice time staring, and did not cry any more.

"Pretty soon the stage stopped at the gate leading to Tillie's home. As her aunt helped the little girl out, the shawl slipped from her hands, and down it fell on the grass.

"'Oh, my child! my child!' she exclaimed, 'you have broken your neck! you have broken your neck! Oh, are you all killed?' Then she began to shriek softly, as if the baby was crying her eyes out, until she saw her mother standing, smiling, at the door of the house, when she began to laugh, and forgetting all about her poor baby, sprang to her arms, looking very much like a dear little baby herself.

"The next day was Sunday. Tillie had been taught to keep it holy. She never wanted to play with her dolls or toys, but liked to go to church with her papa and mamma, and if she did not quite understand all that the good minister said, she always sat very still. The naughty little girl in the next pew would try her best to make Tillie laugh. She would tie knots in the corners of her pocket handkerchief, and roll it into the shape of a little fat man, and dance it up and down before her; but Tillie would not laugh. Then she would twist her face all kinds of ways, run out her tongue, and pretend to be biting the end of it off; but Tillie never so much as smiled. She had been taught the ten commandments by her loving mother, and she knew just as well as you or I what the fourth commandment was, and how to keep it.

"Well, my little kittens, as I was telling you, it was Sunday — bright, beautiful, but quite cold.

"As they went up stairs after breakfast to dress for church, Tillie's aunt said, 'I believe I will wear my black and white blanket shawl, it is so very cold.'

"When she came to take the great black-headed pins out and unfold it — for it was still a big round roll of a baby — she found it was all creased, and tumbled, and looked very bad.

"'Dear me!' said she to herself, 'I ought to have looked at this last night. It was very careless in me.'

"She stood thinking a moment, then went down stairs into the kitchen, and put an iron on the fire. She meant to press out the shawl herself, as the servants might object to ironing on Sunday.

"I am sorry to think that you will know by this that Tillie's aunt did not think of God's holy day and His commandment, as she ought to have done.

"Pretty soon the iron was quite hot. She got out the skirt board, which had been put away in the closet, spread her shawl out smooth, and began to press it back and forth with the hot iron.

"Her back was turned to the open door, and she was so busy over her shawl, that she never heard some tiny little pattering footsteps coming down the stairs; or saw a sweet little child now standing in the doorway.

"It was Tillie, with an expression on her face, half astonishment and half sorrow.

"She looked on for a moment in silence, while the hot iron went back and forth, back and forth. Then she took two or three steps forward, a strange light came into her eyes, one little hand was raised, and then the voice of a child, sorrowful and earnest, uttered these words:Six days shall thou labor, and do all that thou hast to do, but the seventh is the Sabbath of the Lord thy God.

"Tillie's aunt started, and gave a cry as though some one had struck her a violent blow; so awful did this reproof sound from the mouth of a little child. Back went the skirt board and iron into the closet, and the half-smoothed shawl was taken up stairs in silence.

"What could she say? She was breaking the fourth commandment; and she wept bitter tears over her great fault; and I am sure, as long as she lives, she will keep the black and white shawl, and remember that God saw fit, out of the mouth of a child, to reprove her for working on His Holy day."

The little children had listened, without losing a single word; and they understood it all, for Willie exclaimed: "Oh, what a naughty aunt! but she won't do so again, will she, mamma?"

"I know a little hymn about Sunday," said Minnie.

"Well, say it, dear," said the little mother.

"I want to sing it," said Minnie.

"So you shall, dear," answered the mother, "and we will all sing with you."

The dear child's eyes sparkled with pleasure at this, and she began with her sweet robin's note to sing—I am sure every little boy and girl has heard it before—

"Lord, how delightful 'tis to see,A whole assembly worship thee.At once they sing, at once they pray;They hear of heaven, and learn the way.

"I've been to church, and love to go,'Tis like a little heaven below;Not for my pleasures or my play,WOULD I FORGET THE SABBATH DAY."

All the children joined in singing this hymn, with hearts and voices; and their Heavenly Father heard, and poured his blessing down upon this good and happy family.

LITTLE SALLIE'S LONG WORDS.

This evening the mother said: Here is a story Aunt Fanny wrote a long time ago, about Sarah, her daughter, and her niece Fanny. It is true, every word; and she says that she was reminded of it by an anecdote, which a lady told her of one of her own dear little daughters.

The lady said: "Not long ago my Mary was invited to a children's party. I made her a very pretty dress; and just before she went I kissed her and said, 'Now, my darling, you know what a little tear-coat you are—do try this time, if you can come home without a single rent in your pretty frock.'

"'Oh, yes, mamma!' she answered, 'I will take the most paticularest care of it;' and she smoothed it softly down, and walked out with such a funny, mincing step that I had to laugh.

"But the little monkey came home a sight to behold; the dress hung in tatters, as if some wild animal had torn it in pieces.

"'Why!' I exclaimed, 'here's the rag bag walking in.'

"Mary looked in my face with a sweet, sorrowful expression, and tripping close up to me, with a little, dancing step, on the tips of her toes, said, 'Oh, mamma, I met with such a unfortin—I tore my frock; please to excuse me.'

"I had to laugh—and seeing that, she concluded that her 'unfortin' was rather a good joke—and went laughing and singing off to bed.

"But," Aunt Fanny goes on to say, "you dear little darlings, please don't go to tearing your clothes for the fun of it—this winter at least—as we have no time to mend them, while we are working for the brave soldiers.

"After we are at peace, and all happy and comfortable, let's have a grand tearing time together—because we shall be so glad. I promise that you shall tear me into three-cornered pieces, or any other shape you like, when that happy time comes; but now, my darlings, we must wear our old clothes, and save our money to buy comforts for the defenders of the flag. That's my opinion. What's yours? Please let me know in your longest words, and see if I don't print them in a book some of these days. That's all."

A TRUE STORY.

One day little Sallie's mother was very ill indeed; she was lying on the bed with a bandage dipped in ice water around her head, for her head was throbbing and aching as if it were made entirely of double rows of teeth, every one of them afflicted with a jumping, raging toothache, and her little daughter felt so sorry for her, that she begged permission to go to a shop and buy her a new head.

Sallie was an only child; she played little with other children, and she was so accustomed to being constantly with her father and mother, and other grown persons, that she talked in a very amusing and funny fashion, for she would use very long words, perfectly understanding their meaning, but with such comically strange jumblings and twistings, and alterings of syllables, as to make it very difficult to preserve a becoming gravity while listening to her. If you laughed, the fun was all over, for Sallie would turn as red as a whole box of wafers; all the dimples in her face would take French leave, and you could almost have declared there was a bonfire lighted up in each of her eyes; but this only lasted a moment, for she was a sweet-tempered, affectionate little creature, and got over being laughed at as quick as possible, which is a great deal quicker than you or I would have done.

"Dear mamma," said Sallie, her face perfectly beaming with tenderness and sympathy; "dear mamma, what a terrible pain you are in; it is really overpalling! It's very instraordinary that you should have such a head. I can feel the beating! I wish you could sell it to the drummer of a regimen, and buy a new one; I wish I could give you mine, mamma; mine is perfectly empty; not a speck of pain, or anything else, in it, and it would last just so, as long as you live, and ever so much longer. It is so destressing to have a head so brimful of sufferling;" and little Sallie looked as grieved as cock-robin's wife when he was killed by the sparrow, with his bow and arrow.

"My dear dove and darling," said her mother, "I know you would give your head and shoulders, and all your new shoes, to make me well, but you can do nothing but keep perfectly quiet, as still as a mouse with the lock-jaw.

As the Frenchman says, you must 'take hold of your tongue, and put your toe on your mouth;'—he meant finger, I suppose. You need not leave the room, my little Sallie, only do not make any noise."

So Sallie sat down very quietly on the carpet with her kitten, only whispering once in a while, "Play softly, kitty, for your mamma is veryundisposed."

Just at this moment another little girl came darting like a sunbeam into the room. It was Fanny. Fanny was Sallie's cousin; she was a dear little weeny woman of seven years, with a lily-white skin, hazel eyes, and a sweet, musical voice, and she ran up to Sallie with such a gentle, song-like salutation, you would have supposed it was a bob-o-link, saying, "How do you do?" Let me tell you, if you have never heard a bob-o-link, its few low notes are deliciously sweet, and are only surpassed by the sweet voice of a good little girl.

Fanny had come to spend the day with Sallie. She was about a year older than her cousin; she had the same amiable, affectionate ways, and used almost as many long words, so they got on together famously.

It was raining a little, and Fanny said the mud in the streets was very stickery, and she had hard work to keep her boots clean. "I declare," she continued, "such very dirty streets are only fit for esquarians."

"Esquarians!" said Sallie, "what kind of an animal is that? Pigs?"

"My patience!" said Fanny, "did you never hear of esquarian exercise? I take it every day at Mr. Disbrow's. It is riding on horseback."

"Oh!" said Sallie, rubbing her chin, "of course. I was a perfect goose not to know that. I wish, when the streets are muddy, we could fly like birds through the air: how pleasant it must be to be dangling in the air, with nothing to do but stare at the sun! I would not come down for a week. Just fancy! what perfect happiness!"

"And no lessons to learn," said Fanny. "Now, there's grammar—I hate it like pepper, and the hard words in the dictionary nearlydiscolates my jaw. You ought to be thankful, Sallie, that you don't go to school; for my part, I am always glad when 'chatterday' comes, as you call it."

Sallie knew better than that, but she called Saturday chatterday, because Fanny almost always spent that day with her, and they chattered so much you would hardly believe but what they had breakfasted on two or three dictionaries apiece, and each word was undergoing digestion.

"I think I should like to go to Mr. Abbott's school," said Sallie; "mamma says that they have an intermittent of five minutes in every hour. Only think! you can talk to everybody, or walk with anybody, or put your head in your desk, or eat candy, or drink water all the time, or never stop laughing, or anything else you please till the five minutes are over. That's the school for me. I should think he would have a million of scholars. I am sure if I studied all the time, my head would be cracked in a week. Why, Fanny, I tried to say the alphabet backward the other evening, and it fatwigged me so I had to go to bed."

Here Sallie's mother gave a little laugh, which was instantly changed into a smothered groan, for the laughing hurt her head, that it seemed as if a whole regiment of dragoons was galloping through her brain; but the long words and the wrong words sounded so funny, and the children acted and talked so much like two old ladies over a cup of tea, it was not human nature to keep from being amused; and, in fact, their comical prattle acted like a fairy talisman or distant music; it soothed her, and made her in a measure forget her pain.

Sallie heard only the groan, and coming softly to the bed, she whispered: "Dear mamma, did we talk too loud? I meant to be as moute as a muce. I mean as mute as a mouse."

Her mother laughed again at this funny mistake; she could not help it, and Sallie laughed too, and said, "That was a mistake, you know; I had a kink in my tongue; I do believe it must have been twisted like a corkscrew. It is all right now, isn't it, mamma?" and Sallie ran her tongue out till you could nearly see the roots, and it seemed quite wonderful where she kept it all, and that it did not get worn out with all the hard work and exercise she gave it; but I suppose some people's tongues are like dogs' tails, they like to show how happy they are by keeping up a continual wagging.

"Shall we go into the next room and play there?" asked Sallie; "we will be so still you will think the very chairs and tables are taking a nap; we will be like the mummies in the cats' combs, and I should like very much to know what a cats' comb is, and how a mummy can be buried in it."

"You mean cacatombs," laughed little Fanny. "Papa says they are either taverns or caverns — I forget which he said — in Egypt, where they bury the mummies."

"You must call it catacombs, my dear little girls; they are large caverns, not taverns: a mummy in a tavern would frighten all the idlers and ragamuffins out of it. I don't know but what it would be a good plan, but you two dear little twisters and turners of the king's English would frighten that cranky old fellow, Dr. Johnson, into a long sickness, if he was only alive and could hear you. I love to hear you talk; it does me good. Don't go out of the room, but take that pack of cards I gave you to play with, and sit down on the floor and build card houses."

The children thought this a capital idea. Down they sat in great glee, and immediately commenced the business of building houses, their eyes nearly starting out of their heads, in their anxiety to make houses three stories high; but, spite of all their efforts, the moment they attempted the third story, down would come all the cards with a flop, leaving the builders with a long-sounding O — h, to stare at the ruins.

"The fact is," said Sallie, looking so wise and solemn you would have thought she was an owl's granddaughter, at least, "the fact is, there is one peculiarrarity about card houses."

"What's that?" asked Fanny, pursing up her mouth and trying to look as if she knew already.

"Why, I'll tell you," answered Sallie, taking a long breath for the prodigious long word that was coming, "if you ever expect to build card houses, or cocked hats, or steamboats, you must go to work systimystiattically."

"That's not the word," said Fanny, looking as dignified as ten judges; "that's not the word at all, Sallie."

"What is it, then?" said Sallie, shutting one eye, and looking very hard at Fanny with the other.

"Sister Mister Macalley! There! don't I know?"

"My dear child," answered Sallie, with a patronizing air, and her head on one side, "you are right. It is Sister Mister Macalley; I only said systimystiattically for fun, you know—just for fun and fancy, old Aunt Nancy." And the little girls laughed merrily, and thought it a capital joke.

Sallie's mother had to laugh too, until she was almost killed, at this last sally. She did not wonder that the long word "systematically" had proved one too many for the children; she expected, the next thing, to hear of "indivisibility," or "incompatibility," or something twice as long, if possible; but, at any rate, the laughing or something else did her so much good that she felt well enough to get up and drink a cup of tea and eat a piece of dry toast, while the little girls were having their luncheon, and desperate were the efforts she was obliged to make, to keep from laughing at the speeches they made over the meal. They were twenty times more amusing than the heavy, long-winded jokes with which aldermen, and other big bugs entertain each other for hours at the great public dinners, where they are obliged to give each other the wink to let every one know where the laugh ought to come in. No! it was just one little, rollicking, chuckling laugh all lunch time; and how they managed to make so much bread and butter and raspberry jam disappear, I am sure I cannot tell.

Sallie lived in the city of New York, in Eleventh street, very near Broadway. Directly round the corner was Mrs. Wagner's ice cream saloon, or, as Sallie called it, "Mrs. Waggles."

In the afternoon her mother said she and Fanny might go, by themselves, to this saloon, and buy each a treat of six-pence worth of ice cream.

The children were in a perfect ecstasy of delight at this announcement; their faces were radiant with good humor and happiness. Only to think of it! what grandeur! to go all by themselves! that was the great point! not a cousin, or a grandmother, or even a nurse to take care of them; and they scrabbled up on all the chairs, and jumped down again, and twirled round and round till Sallie's mother said it was fortunate their heads, and arms, and legs were all fastened together very strong, or they would long ago have been whirled off their bodies, and out of the windows.

I wish you could have seen Sallie having her hair curled that afternoon. Her mother would be in the act of laying a curl gracefully over one ear, when Sallie's head would bob suddenly round, and the curl would be planted right between her eyes, making her squint dreadfully; and when a curl was to repose on her temple, Sallie would bob the other way, and the curl would be landed on the back of her head, the end sticking up like a horn. She did try, but who could keep still, on such a delightful occasion, when they were going to walk about the world just like grown people, with their money in their pockets! Sallie even wanted her mother to lend her a lace veil, and her gold watch, to add to her dignity—"so as to come home in time for tea, you know, mamma;" but her mother concluded, as Sallie could not tell the time by the watch, the necessity for carrying it was rather doubtful. And after considerable tumbling and popping around like fire-crackers, and making cheeses and whirligigs, and chattering like a whole army of magpies, the children were dressed, at last, and sent on their way rejoicing.

When they got into the street, they took hold of each other's hands and ran all the way, as an inevitable matter of course, and arrived at the ice cream saloon in a laughing, breathless condition, so very little like grown people that I am afraid they must have forgotten their dignity, or left it locked up in the bookcase at home.

They took their seats at one of the marble tables, and with very large eyes and innumerable giggles gave their order, and then there never before was such splendid ice cream! It was so cold, they really had to blow it, and they had to stop a great many times to laugh, and to wonder what the other people thought of them; at any rate, everybody would think they were "instraordinary" good girls to be allowed to come out all by themselves.

"Only imagine," continued Sallie, "perhaps, after this, we shall be considit such excellent children—kind of oldey and serious, you know—that mamma will pack up our trunks, and let us go eleventeen times farther than this. How perfectly delightful! to go in every direction at once, and rush all round the world like the comic papa told me of the other day;" and Sallie became so excited with this brilliant prospect that she jumped up and down, and gave a little scream of joy.

"What's all that noise?" said a queer, discordant voice at the farther end of the saloon.

The children started, and looked back a little frightened; their charming castles in the air put to flight, "like the baseless fabric of a vision," by the rough question which they thought had been aimed at them.

"Walk in, ladies! take a seat! What will you have? Shut up! G-o-o-d morning!"

The words sounded as if they had been rubbed through a nutmeg grater.

"Take a piece of pie? don't forget to pay for it! Shut up! Call again! I'm all right! Hurra!" And the parrot—for it was a large and handsome parrot— hopped upon a chair, from the floor where he had been strutting about, and looked at the company with eyes as sharp as a carving-knife.

Fanny and Sallie, by this time, had found out that it was a bird that was talking to them, and not cross old Mr. Grumpy, as they had at first supposed, who, always being in an ill humor himself, never could bear to see any one looking happy. They walked up to where the bird was, and stood there lost in admiration at his accomplishments; and really he was a very wonderful bird, and sometimes talked as if he understood what he was saying, which, between you and me, is what some birds, boobies for instance, cannot do.

While they were standing there as still as could be expected, for they had to give a little skip now and then, under such remarkable circumstances, a nurse came up with a very beautiful baby in her arms, and two young gentlemen also drew near to listen to the parrot. As soon as Poll saw the baby, he yelled out: "Sweet little baby! sweet little baby! G-o-o-d morning, little baby! Is it a girl?"

The nurse, who was a very silly-looking goose of a girl, turned very red at this question, and, dropping a courtesy to Poll, simpered out: "No, sir; if yez plaze, sir, it's a boy, sir!" A roar of laughter from all around followed this answer, and the poor girl looked as if she thought the parrot was a police officer, in a bright-green great coat, who meant to put her instantly to death for daring to answer him. She concluded she had better run for her life, which she accordingly did, stumbling against all the tables, and breaking her toes over every chair; but she disappeared at last, the parrot shrieking most horribly after her, and all the people laughing till their sides ached.

With many a lingering, admiring glance at their funny new friend, the children at last left the enchanting saloon, and hastened home to tell of all the wonderful things they had seen and heard; both talking, exclaiming, and laughing at once, until it would have taken at least six mammas to have heard it all.

When Sallie's father came home, of course he had to hear how they went out, "just like two old women, very independent, and eat a poll parrot and heard an ice cream," at which he was greatly astonished until they explained that it was the ice cream they had eaten, and the poll parrot they had heard.

Soon after tea, Fanny was sent for, and after many attempts, her bonnet and pretty little white Marseilles cloak were fastened, for she jumped, and Sallie jumped during the operation, till you would have thought they were pith witches, only they fortunately kept on their feet; afterward they kissed each other jumping, and the kisses lighted on the very ends of their noses, and Sallie ran to the corner with her, and bade her good-by, and ran back to her mother, who was standing at the door, and ran into the parlor and all round it with such a hop-skip-and-jump, that her mother thought the mayor of the city, if he only could see her, would be wanting to hire her for a lamplighter.

At last the time came for Sallie to go to bed, and she was undressed with plenty more laughing and jumping, but her dear little face grew sober and sweetly serious when she said her prayers, and in this her mother was very particular: not a word was mispronounced; and every syllable was distinctly repeated until the little girl knew them all correctly, and what was more, understood them, and it was a beautiful sight to see the little one's clasped hands and innocent face when she asked God to bless all her relatives and friends, and make her a good child.

Sallie's mother, that evening, seemed to want a great many things out of the nursery; she was continually coming in with a light, and looking for her pocket handkerchief, or thimble, or a book.

At last Sallie grew quite impatient at these disturbances; she sat up straight in her little crib, and in a plaintive tone, said, "Dear mamma, why do you come in so often with a light? you invaluably wake me up when you do."

Her mother rushed out of the room, light and all, to have a laugh over the long word "invariably," which her little Sallie had heard somewhere, and altered so comically, then returning, she kissed the little rosy cheek, and said she really would not disturb her again if she wanted anything ever so much; and with a kiss on the other cheek, as Sallie said, to make it "valance," she bade her good night.

THE NEW LITTLE FRIEND.

"Oh! here is something from Aunt Fanny, which looks extremely interesting," said the little mother one evening.

"Read it, do, please!" cried the children with sparkling eyes. "We will work at our mittens harder than ever, for anything so very nice."

So the kind mother began as follows:

MY DEAR CHILDREN—

I must tell you what happened to me this morning—not for the first time, to be sure; but as it always makes me just as happy, I might as well call them all "first times."

I was very busy writing a ridiculous story for you about the Honorable Mr. Kite, when a barouche full of ladies drove up to the door. As I was sitting at the window, I could see them getting out. With them was a lovely little girl.

"Oh!" said I to Sarah, my daughter, "what a darling little child is coming here! I never saw her or the ladies before, and I am afraid they have stopped at the wrong house."

But the front door bell rang, and a moment after the servant handed me two cards. One was quite large and almost square. It had the name of a lady upon it. The other was such a dear little card that I must give you the exact pattern. Here it is—

name and all; and when Maria handed it to me, she said, "Oh, ma'am! if you could only see what a sweet little girl is down stairs! She took this card out of a silver card case of about the same size as this, and she smiled and skipped into the house as if she was sopleased!"

You may be sure I was not long in going down to the parlor. I had hardly got in the door when two little arms were round me, and a sweet voice said, "Aunt Fanny;" and when I stooped down, I think I got at least twenty kisses. Then one of the ladies took my hand, and told me how her little daughter loved me, and, above all, loved "Lame Charley," because she, like him, had been very ill for a long time, and his patience and sweetness had helped her to be patient and sweet. "But my darling is better now," she continued; "and when we came to New York, she begged me to bring her to see you."

I came very near crying. A thankful prayer rose in my heart, that God had permitted me to add to the happiness of this little one, whose pale, delicate face showed that she had passed through much suffering. It does grieve me so, to know that children must sometimes spend hours and days in pain! And I stooped again and kissed this tender little blossom, and felt sure, as I looked at the soft, loving expression of her large dark eyes, that Jesus, our Saviour and Friend, had loved and comforted her all through her illness.

The other lady was her aunt—a gentle, lovely person, for whom I seemed to feel an affection at once: indeed, we all talked together like old friends, and I could hardly bear to have them go away. I had a strange feeling, as if I must have known them all before, in some far off time. The mother's voice especially had a charming, cordial tone, which I shall always remember.

They could not stay very long, they said, because they had left a lady in the carriage who was an invalid. Then I wanted to run out and bring her in; but they said they must go; and my dear little new friend left me, with kisses, and promises to come some time and see me again.

This visit put me in mind of a story about little Annie, which I meant to have told you before. If you will please to forgive me, I will tell it to you now. I shall call it "Ilken Annie," because that is her own name for herself. By "ilken" she means "little."

ILKEN ANNIE.

Ilken Annie lives in a beautiful house on Staten Island. Her mamma and I are great friends, and we have had plenty of pleasant fun together. Near the house is a lovely little lake, shaped exactly like the figure "eight" turned sideways, so: [symbol]. It has a cunning little bridge in the narrowest part, across which a whole regiment of dolls could march—and you and I, too, for that matter. It is so small and pretty, that I do believe you and I could catch gold fish out of it. I have looked very hard in it to find a mermaid, which, you know, is a lady with no feet: instead of those, she has a fish's tail. I wonder how one would taste boiled; for she is only a fish, after all, like the sea horses which swim about in the aquarium at Barnum's Museum. If Annie and I ever catch a mermaid in this beautiful lake, we will be sure to tell you all about it.

Near by is a grand old oak tree, standing alone and majestic, like a king on his throne; and a lovely flower garden, at the side of the house, is so bright in colors that one would suppose a company of rainbows had gone to housekeeping there.

In the middle of this garden there stands, day and night, a beautiful young lady, in a round straw hat; but I wouldn't kiss her for a dollar! for her cheeks, as well as all the rest of her, are as white as chalk and as hard as a stone. I dare say her heart is too, if she happens to have any. Who wants to kiss stone people? I'd rather kiss you, and ilken Annie, and that other sweet little Annie who came to see me.

Ilken Annie, when she was about four years old, was one pleasant day sitting in her chair by the window, knitting a little white garter — that is, she was learning to knit one.

"Oh my," she said, "the stitch is so naughty! It is running away! What shall I do?"

You see, there were five stitches on the knitting needle, and Annie's little fat fingers had hard work to keep them there.

So her kind mamma showed her very carefully how to pull a stitch through with the other needle, before it had time to be off on its travels; and the dear little child, with a bright smile, kissed her mother, and said, "It is all tight now; oh, how glad I am!" And she put out her chubby little leg to try how much larger that celebrated stitch had made the garter.

Presently she cried out again, "Oh, mamma, here's a stitch all climbed up, and another all rolled down; and one is so little I can't see his eye to poke the needle through. Oh, what a bad children!"

Her mother laughed at this funny speech, and said pleasantly, "'Try, try again,' ilken Annie." Then she pulled and twitched at the "bad children-stitches;" and once more Annie sat down to knit, singing, with a pretty little bird's note—

"'Tis a lesson you should heed:Try, try again;If at first you don't succeed,Try, try again."

Of course you know all of this pretty little song, don't you? Just sing it now.

By and by the little girl and her mother went down to luncheon; and there, on the table, were such lots of nice cream and raspberries, and white home-made bread! Oh! how I wish all the darling children in the world could have such a delicious lunch—so much better for them than pies or a whole bushel of sugar candy.

When this nice lunch was over, Annie's mother said, "My little darling, I am going to New York to buy a chest of tea, and hire a cook, besides taking a trunk which belongs to a friend. You must keep house for me, dear; and if any company comes, behave very politely to them, and take off their bonnets, and talk to them, and ask them to stay till I come home."

"So ilken Annie will, mamma," she answered; "but I'll tell them they mustn't pull off their shoes and stockings and paddle in the lake, saying, 'quack,' and making believe they are a duck, like brother did. I'll tell them that's naughty, won't I?"

"Yes," said the good mamma, laughing, "tell them what brother did. That will amuse them very much, dear; and when I come home, I will give you a dozen kisses and a pretty new book."

Oh, how Annie's blue eyes sparkled at this! for, would you believe it, she could read! Yes, read! and only four years old! It did not seem to have hurt her; for she was just as round, and plump, and rosy as possible. She learned her letters, nobody knows how—from the topsof newspapers; and the reading came so easy, that instead of having to learn in that pretty little school book called, "Reading without tears," Annie seemed always to have on a ticklesome apron, which turned all her lessons into "reading with laughing;" and it was such a funny business, and Annie grew so fat and bright under it, that her mother did not feel worried; but I advise all the rest of you, little darlings, if you don't like learning to read quite as well as bread and butter and raspberry jam, to put it off till your dear little heads and bodies have had at least two years more of play, and frolic, and tumbling about like kittens. You like that advice, don't you?

So Annie helped her mother to dress. She ran to the closet, brought out a green bandbox, and raising the cover, lifted up her mother's bonnet; then she opened one of the bureau drawers, and got her a pair of new kid gloves, and shut the drawer again. "Oh!" cried she, with a little laugh, "I forgot to take out a clean hankfun—too bad!" By this funny word she meant "pocket handkerchief."

So she ran back to the bureau, opened the drawer, and took a "hankfun" from a pile in the corner; and then her mother was quite ready.

Annie felt a little bit like crying when her mamma kissed her for good-by. She was such a little thing, you see—only four years old. Youdon't want your mamma to go away either, do you? you precious little rose, pink, bluebell, daisy!

But ilken Annie tried to look pleasant, and that is a famous way to be pleasant.

The carriage was just driving away, when the little girl remembered that her mother had not taken a shawl. It might be quite cool by the afternoon; so she ran quickly up stairs, got a plaid shawl, and Harry, one of her brothers, who is a right handsome little fellow, and as good as he is handsome, ran to the carriage with it; and then kissed his hand and raised his cap to his mamma for good-by; while Archie, the coachman, was looking on in great admiration.

Then he drove away with her, down to the Hunchback, at the landing, which was to take her to New York.

Now, don't you think, you fanny darling, that the "Hunchback" was an old man with a great lump on his shoulders; and Annie's mother was to take a seat on the top of it; and then the old man would swim to New York with her. Not a bit of it! The Hunchback was only an ugly old steamboat, which was all hunched up in the middle; and scratched through the water like a great crab trying to dance the polka.

Annie sat down and began to knit a little.

While she was knitting, she said this funny thing, which Eliza, the nurse, had taught her. See if you can say it:

"Little Kitty Kickshaw knotted and knitted for her kith and kinsfolk in her kinsman's kitchen.

"This knotting and knitting by little Kitty Kickshaw, in her kinsman's kitchen, kept her kinsfolk.

"So come and kiss kind little Kitty Kickshaw, for keeping her kith and kinsfolk by knotting and knitting in her kinsman's kitchen."

Pretty soon, down dropped a stitch off the needle.

"O—h," said Annie, "too bad! I must put it away till mamma comes home." So she opened a drawer in the table and laid her knitting down. Then she put on a nice little pink sun bonnet, and ran out into the garden to pick some flowers. The stone young lady smiled at her; but as she could not speak or run, Annie did not care a speck for her: she thought a great deal more of the good little dog dozing on the mat before the door.

Pretty soon the dog, whose name was Grip, woke up, shook himself, and ran after her to have a frolic, for he was always ready for that; and Annie and he raced around, till her sun-bonnet fell off. Then she sat down under the grand old oak tree, and had a real nice talk with Grip, who ran out his tongue, and wagged his tail, and looked as wise as Solomon.

He was just listening very attentively to a story about the beautiful new house her papa had had built for the ducks to live in, when there came a sound like the crunching of wheels on the gravelled road; and in a twinkling he cocked up his ears, and, without waiting for the end of the story, ran off barking, to see who had arrived. I think he was very impolite; don't you?

Then Annie got up and ran too, saying to herself, "Why! I wonder if dear mamma has come back."

No; it was not her mother's carriage. It was another one; and it soon whirled round the sweep, and stopped at the door.

"Oh, my," said Annie, "that is the company. I must go and help her out. Why, grandmamma!" she exclaimed, "dear grandmamma, is that you?"

"Yes, little darling," said a pleasant voice; and a tall, beautiful lady stepped from the carriage, and lifting Annie in her arms, gave her a good kissing.

"Oh, grandmamma, I'm so glad. I am the house-keeping; and I must be very polite and kind to you. Come in, grandmamma, and let me take off your hat."

The lady sat down in the parlor, smiling at the sweet little child, and let her untie her bonnet with her small fat fingers. It took quite a long time, for Annie could not get the right ribbon to pull; but her grandmamma never said "hurry," but let the little one do just as she pleased.

"Mamma has gone to New York, grandma," said Annie, "to buy a cook and hire a chest of tea."

"Buy a cook?" asked her grandma, laughing.

"Oh, yes, grandma," said Annie, quite serious; "she told me so."

"Hire a cook and buy the tea. Isn't that it, darling?"

"O—h, yes, grandma! I made a mistake, didn't I?"

They both laughed merrily, and then Annie, sitting in her own tiny chair, put one little fat hand over the other, and began to think.

She looked up at her kind, beautiful grandma, with such a serious pair of blue eyes, that the good lady came near laughing; but she sat quite still, to see what Annie would do or say next. She loved the little girl dearly.

You see, Annie was such a loving, obedient little child, that she was anxious to do just what her mother told her; and she was thinking of the best way to be kind to the company.

Suddenly her blue eyes brightened, as if she had got hold of a delightful thought; and looking up, with the expression of an angel, in her grandmother's face, she said, in her sweet little voice, "Grandma, shall I read the Bible to you?"

"Oh, the precious child!" Truly, "of such is the kingdom of heaven."

Her grandmother's eyes filled with happy tears as she said, "Yes, darling;" and ilken Annie, getting her own pretty Bible, read about good little Samuel to her grandmother.

Then she got into her lap, and sang her ever so many little songs; and let me tell you, that anybody would have wished to be a grandmother right away, if they could have had such a delightful time as Annie's grandmother did. I'm sure I do.

And when the dear mamma came home, and heard all that her sweet little child had done, she took her in her arms and fondly kissed her, and prayed God in her heart that He would make her "ilken" Annie always as good and lovely as she was then. I am almost certain she will be; for a good child will be sure to become a good woman or man. So take care, little darlings, to be better than ever you were before; and above all, obedient to your parents.

Not long after this, a great event happened at Annie's house. You must know that she had no less than five loving brothers; all older than herself. Quite a lot of them, isn't there? And their mother let them have all manner of innocent fun and frolic; because she was one of the very best mothers in the world, and knew that children ought to be made not only as good, but as happy as possible. So, lo and behold! everybody and his wife, and I too, were invited to a splendid concert at Annie's house.

The best of it was, that the concert was to be just like Christy's minstrels; and the boys, and some of their friends who were to help, had bought the most splendid black woolly wigs; and were going to have their faces made very nearly as black as ink. I tell you what it is! I was just as full of the fun of it as I could hold; and I went directly to a jeweller I knew, and got him to lend me several breastpins, with such big make-believe diamonds in them, that they almost put your eyes out shining. These the boys wore in their ruffled shirts; and they were such dandies! oh my, what dandies they were!

You must know, at a real concert, the people throw beautiful flowers to the singers that please them most. Annie and I got up an immense bouquet, about the size of a peck measure, without telling anybody a word about it; and saved it up, to throw at one of the "colored gemmen."

The evening came, and was warm and clear; little Alice and the "Doctor," my two children and I went early. As we drove in at the gate it looked like fairy land; for, hanging to the trees in every direction, were beautiful colored Chinese lanterns; the long winding drive to the house was all a-light with them.

A band of music was playing on the wide piazza; and as we entered, everybody was presented with a beautiful red, white, or blue paper fan. Wasn't it splendid?

How little Annie's eyes did sparkle! they were like real diamonds, and far more precious. She nestled down in a seat close to me, and together we enjoyed all the comical songs and funny jokes of the minstrels.

You don't know how queer their black wigs looked! and they kept Annie and me laughing all the time, with rolling their eyes, making funny faces, and telling conundrums.

Presently Willie, one of Annie's brothers, who played the bones, called out to Robert, a neighbor's son, who was banging the tamborine on his head and his elbow, and his knee and his foot, as fast and as hard as he could.

"Mister Julius."

"What dat you want, Mister Snow?"

"You know dat ar ole saw you lent me, Mister Julius, to saw de dictionary in two, so to gib you half?"

"Yes, sar, I know him very well, sar."

"Well, sar, dat ar saw, sar, he wort nottin, sar! Ob all de saws dat I ebber saw saw, I nebber saw a saw saw as dat ar saw saws! He! ho!"

"I don't see dat ar saw, sar; but I want to ax you a question."

"Berry well; succeed."

"When de day breaks, what becomes ob de pieces?"

"I—I—don't 'xactly know, sar. Trow em in de ash barrel?"

"No, sar! dey jes let em alone. He! ho!"

Then another brother got up, and made such a low bow that his black wig tumbled over his eyes, showing his brown hair behind. He poked it back again, and began to sing this—all the rest playing on fiddles, bones, and triangles, as hard as they could:

"Come, brothers, now unite with us, and join us, one and all,The Stars and Stripes shall not come down, shall never, never fall:We've got two splendid captains, to their country ever true;McClellan, and great Winfield Scott, and the Red, White, and Blue.

Chorus. "Then hurrah for the Union,Hurrah for the Union,Hurrah for the Union,And the Red, White, and Blue."

"Ah! now's the time for the bouquet!" I whispered to Annie; and I took it out from under the seat, and threw it as hard as I could. The little dog who lived with Annie, thought I did it for him to catch. He bounced upon the stage, barking and wagging his tail till he nearly wagged it off; and seized the bouquet, while Annie's brother tried to get it away; and they chased each other up and down the room, the minstrels and the company all laughing ready to kill themselves. What fun it was!

At last Annie's brother got about a quarter of the flowers away from the dog; and then he put his hand on his heart, and made a bow lower than the first; and Annie was afraid he had almost broken the bone in his back.

After this funny concert was over, the musicians, who had been sent for from New York, began to play dancing tunes; and all the company went into another large parlor, and commenced to dance; while Annie's brothers and their friends got scrubbing brushes, and soap, and hot water, and scrubbed and rubbed, and scrubbed and rubbed, till they nearly scrubbed the noses off their faces; but it was not very long before they came in, looking as white and clean as could be; only Annie thought they had made a great mistake—taking out their splendid breastpins. She said, "Why, Aunt Fanny, those breastpins are so brighty bright! oh, how I wish I had one! Don't you?"

"Yes, dear," I answered; "and I will go and ask the jeweller to give me one for you to keep. You shall choose it yourself."

This was delightful! and Annie and I danced and laughed, and had some ice cream in a snug little corner together; and she sat up ever so late, without wanting to shut her blue eyes once; and when the company went away they kissed Annie, and shook hands with the handsome, gentlemanly little boys, and thanked them for their nice, funny concert. I don't know but what some of them kissed one or two of the youngest of Annie's brothers. I did; but that's because I'm only Aunt Fanny, which makes a difference, you see. I'm so little, that half the time the children forget I am quite old. They catch hold of me, and make me play so hard, that I am afraid I shall never get to be a very mouldy old lady, sitting in a corner, with my head tied up in a flannel petticoat, to keep off the draught. I'm afraid I shall always be frisky. What do you think about it, you little apple dumplings?

Would you like to hear the rest about the breastpin? Well, I will tell you. Annie chose the one with the great red stone in the middle and ten white ones all round it; and I went the very next day to the jeweller in New York, and said:

"See here, Mr. Jeweller, here are all your breastpins, and I am very much obliged to you; but I want you to give me one, for a darling."

"What kind of a darling, Mrs. Aunt Fanny?"

"Well, she is four years old, and has rosy cheeks, dark brown hair, large blue eyes, and a little dimpling, dainty mouth, full of small white pearls. They are not set in gold, like the pearls in your glass case. No, indeed! they grew fast in her dear little head; and she eats bread and milk with them.

"But let me tell you, Mr. Jeweller, that she has something far more precious than what I have been relating. Shut up in her innocent breast is a beautiful heart, which is full of love to all around her; and it gently whispers to her, 'Ilken Annie, be obedient to your parents, kind to everybody, and faithful in praying night and morning, to the dear Saviour, to watch over and protect His little lamb, and all she loves.' Oh, Mr. Jeweller, you cannot find such a precious jewel as ilken Annie's heart, in all your store."

Something came into the good jeweller's eyes, and fell upon his cheeks. They were two bright tears; and he softly said, "No; I have no such treasures here, and none now in my home; for, not long ago, God took my one little white lamb, my wee darling. She has gone to heaven, and my house is empty."

I felt very, very sorry for him—but I could not speak. He wrapped up the breastpin in a piece of paper, and gave it to me for Annie; and I sent it to her with this fine poetry:

My dear "ilken" Annie,Your loving Aunt FannyHas got this fine breastpinOn purpose for you;So that, when in town,With your new hat and gown,And this red and white breastpin,You'll be quite a view.

Then the girls and the boysWill make a great noise,And cry, "Goody gracious!What a breastpin! just see!'Tis the color of roses!And real, I supposes;I wish your Aunt FannyWould buy one for me."

Then you'll say, "But she can't,For she isn't your aunt,But my little auntieThat lives down the lane; And I'm ilken Annie,So winsome and cannie,With my 'hankfun' and 'too bad!"And try, try again.'

"I have a dear màmma,And good and grave pàpa,And such a kind grandmamma,Gentle and sweet,And my three, four, five brothers,Like three, four, five mothers,To love me and tend me,And guide my young feet."

And now, little maiden,With so much love laden,I pray that to youMay all "good gifts" be given;And happiness rare,Without shadow of care;And then—this life ended,Your home may be—HEAVEN.

And so ilken Annie got her breastpin from me; and I received in return some kisses from her; and I think I had the best of the bargain. And what is more—I do believe, if you will go down to Staten Island and call upon her, she will show you the garters, which must be finished by this time; and the breastpin, if it isn't lost; and the poetry; and Grip, the dog; and the stone young lady in the garden; and the cunning little bridge; and ever so many dimples in her sweet face; and be so kind to you! Perhaps she will say, "Shall I read the Bible to you." Wouldn't that be lovely? Come! let's you and

I go down together, this very minute! Oh, dear me! I quite forgot that the boats don't run in the evening. Never mind! we'll go some other time.

Till then, don't quite forget

Your loving

AUNT FANNY.

When the reading of these little stories was finished, it was found that twelve more pairs of nice warm mittens were ready for our brave soldiers; and the Little Mother sent them to George, with so much love, and so many prayers for his welfare, and the safety of his comrades—that it did seem as if God's blessing would rest upon every soldier who wore them.

And now, little darling, reading this, or having a kind mamma or friend to read it to you—won't you pray for the soldiers? Will you say this little prayer to-night:

"O my Heavenly Father: Please watch over all the soldiers. Send Thy Holy Spirit into their leaders: then love and peace will surely come; and there will be no more of this dreadful war. I pray for this, in the name of Jesus, my dear Saviour. Amen."

END OF THE SECOND BOOK.